IN DUE SEASON

This is a work of fiction from the authors and are not meant to depict, portray, or represent any particular person. Names, characters, places, and incidents are either the product of the author's imagination or are used fictitiously, and any resemblances to an actual person living or dead are entirely coincidental.

In Due Season

Khara Campbell

Synopsis

Thirty-three-year-old Antwain Hall felt he had no choice but to lean on his faith in God when his world was tossed upside down. Forty-five-year-old Tanya Freeman, on the other hand, had walked away from her faith because she felt it no longer served its purpose in her life – her prayers had gone unanswered for years. She finally come to realize that God's timing is far different from her own. Everything happens in due season, which is when Antwain's and Tanya's lives cross paths.

PLEASE NOTE:

This is Christian fiction with imperfect characters, some of which are still growing in their faith. A few scenarios in the story may be taboo for some readers. Please keep in mind that everyone's journey to faith is different and unique. The situations presented in this work of fiction don't necessarily represent the belief of the author.

1
TANYA

"How does that taste, baby?" A handsome is smile plastered on his face as he pulls the fork away from my mouth.

I chew the tender steak, swallow, then smile deviously. "It's the best meat I've had so far, but I think you have something even better to offer." I lick my lips with my eyes darted towards his jean clad crotch.

"You're not ready for that meat yet, baby. It will uproot your entire world." He smirks while taking a step back from me, sitting at my kitchen island.

"I'm ready!" I pout, folding my arms defiantly. You would think I was a four-year-old child and not a forty-five-year-old woman by the way I'm acting. But I know what I want and it's him! "I want you to uproot my world. I wanna ride, suck, rub, all on that–"

"You're not ready yet, Tanya."

"Yes, I am, Pastor Antwain!"

"...Oh my gawd!" I shout as I wake up from another one of my sexual dreams. I pull my body up into a sitting position on my bed. "I'm going to hell with gasoline lingerie on." I groan while face palming myself.

Ever since I rededicated my life to Christ eight months ago, I've been dreaming about sex often. You would think I was a teenager in heat. And tonight's dream just happened to feature Pastor Antwain Hall. I gave up sex almost two years ago because I grew tired of casual sex with meaningless men. Why didn't I have sex dreams then? Why did it have to start eight months ago, after I restarted my journey of faith? Matthew 16:23 comes to the forefront of my mind. *"Get behind me, Satan! You are a hindrance to me. For you are not setting your mind on the things of God, but on the things of man."*

Most of my teens and all of my twenties, I was a devout Christian, then I went buck wild in my thirties. I gave my life to Christ after I had an abortion at sixteen. The guilt from it sent me straight to the

Lord. My first time having sex and I ended up pregnant. I never told my parents. My boyfriend at the time had a family member who did illegal abortions, so he took me to her. It was successful.

But years later, I realized it wasn't. It messed my reproductive organs up to where I'm unable to carry a child to full term. I've suffered three miscarriages over the years. Along with failed relationships. I grew tired of "living right" when I felt it wasn't profiting me anything. When I turned thirty, I turned my back on my faith. All my prayers for a husband and baby weren't answered, so what was the point? Despite my rebellion, I'm thankful God never gave up on me. He welcomed me back with open arms.

"Ugh! Lord, help Your child." I climb out of bed, going to my adjoined bathroom to relieve my bladder. Of all the men I could've dreamt about, it had to be a pastor.

Returning to the comfort of my queen-sized bed, I check the time on my cellphone on the nightstand. 1:43 on this Sunday morning. If I'm to make the 9 o'clock service, I need to get back to sleep. I lay my head against my firm pillow, hoping I don't continue my dream of Pastor Antwain with his dark chocolate self.

House of Praise is in Accokeek, Maryland, twenty minutes from my house. Today's service blessed me like the others. Pastor Antwain taught about choosing the right tribe of people for your life. I gather my clutch and Bible to make my way out of the sanctuary. I stop and talk briefly to a few people who greet me as I pass by.

I've noticed since my first visit four weeks ago that after service, Pastor Antwain always greets the congregation with either his father, mother, sister or all three at his side. And I can tell why. Women either subtly or boldly throw themselves at him. He is just that fine where women can easily lose their minds— even in the house of the Lord. He has the actor, Kofi

Siriboe's, vibe on lock. Pastor Antwain doesn't look at the women lustfully, graciously putting them in their place in the name of Jesus. Which makes me admire him more.

I groan internally as I walk towards him and his mother standing near one of the church exits. I know I probably shouldn't have a crush on a man of the cloth. And certainly not one twelve years my junior – yet I do. He mentioned his age during last week's sermon. The anointing I feel that's on his life is profound. *Lord, he definitely has the gift of teaching.* Though I wasn't in church in my thirties and some of my forties, I have enough biblical knowledge to identify one of God's disciples.

After waiting for a while, the crowd has died down, giving me my chance to officially meet Pastor Antwain Hall. I will work on tapering down my attraction to him because I need this man as my pastor. In the past few weeks, his teaching has significantly boosted my faith.

"I have a roast cooking in my crock pot. You're more than welcome to stop by for a plate," an extremely attractive sista dressed for the runway says solicitously.

Mrs. Hall not so discreetly rolls her eyes at the comment. I'm guessing she's in her mid-sixties and wears it well. She dresses like a typical church mother with matching hats for all her outfits.

"Not when your intention is for no good. You're not going to lure me into a trap, Sister Corine. Don't ask me again," Pastor Antwain says with finality. Then his face breaks into a warm smile, maybe to help ease her bruise.

Sister Corine clears her throat. I'm sure she feels thoroughly chastised. Apparently, this isn't the first time she's tried to proposition him. I understand her attraction, but it's inappropriate to try to tempt him, especially when he's not interested. This solidifies my stance on not acting on my attraction for him.

This baby...*now you know ain't nothing baby about him. Stop capping. Ugh!*

"I – I didn't...sorry. It won't happen again." Corine hightails it out the doorway without waiting a response.

Two sets of eyes rest upon me. I immediately start to feel self-conscious. *Do I have a booger in my nose?* Maybe it's wishful thinking, or my imagination, but Antwain's eyes sweep over me in a way a pastor's shouldn't. A swarm of butterflies flutters in my belly. Why does this man affect me so?

"Good morning, did you enjoy today's message?" His rich baritone voice floats through the air. He looks even better up close with his full beard and well-groomed, kinky tapered fro. He smells heavenly too. Suits are made just for his physique. I'm 5 feet 5 inches tall. He must be over six feet.

He and his mother anticipate my response, but I'm at a loss for words. I open my mouth to speak, yet nothing comes out. I don't like that this young man has my grown behind speechless, just from the way he looks at me.

Get it together, Tanya Freeman! You are old enough to be his rich auntie.

"Today's sermon and the past three Sunday's sermons have been quite inspiring. I heard you on the radio a few weeks ago and decided to attend in person. You have God's anointing on your life *young man.*"

Pastor Antwain's eyes shine with amusement at my signifying our age difference. He extends his hand in greeting. "Well, *young* lady –"

"Sister Tanya," I interject. My hand is swallowed by his and I try hard not to swoon as he gives it a gentle squeeze before I pull my hand away from his grasp.

"Miss Tanya, welcome to House of Praise. This is my mother, Mrs. Ingrid Hall."

I extend my hand in greeting to Mrs. Hall with my mind still stuck on the fact that Pastor Antwain addressed me as Miss Tanya, not Sister like he does other women as I've noticed over a short period of time.

Mrs. Hall playfully swats my hand away, pulling me into a warm hug. "Welcome. We've been waiting on you for a long time." What does she mean? Have they noticed me dodging greeting them after services the past few weeks?

"Thank you. It's nice to meet you both. I plan on becoming a member of the church," I state after our embrace.

Mrs. Hall claps her hands excitedly. "Wonderful! We're glad to have you...I'm going to get the twins from Children's church, Antwain. Maybe you can tell Tanya about membership class." Mrs. Hall walks away before he replies.

Interesting.

Suddenly there's a shift in the air. It no longer feels as if I'm standing before Pastor Hall. I'm standing before Antwain – the man. We're two of a few people left in the church foyer since church let out about forty-five minutes ago. There's only one Sunday service which means it's time to lock the doors soon.

"New members class is the first Sunday of the month. The next one is April 3rd at one." His gaze feels like kisses all over my face.

Today is March 20th which means the class is in two weeks.

I subconsciously lick my lip-glossed lips. "Do you teach the class?"

"I do." He blesses me with his signature megawatt smile.

"I'll be there," I find myself flirting.

What happened to you tapering your attraction?

Antwain chuckles.

Come on, is there anything unattractive about this man?

"Okay. I hope you enjoy the rest of your Sunday, Miss Tanya."

"You too. Thanks." I do a Corine and hightail it out of there before I do something stupid like tongue kiss him in the Lord's church.

I'm gonna need to bathe in anointing oil and holy water to curb my attraction to him.

2
ANTWAIN

I shake my head in awe as I watch Tanya walk out the church foyer to the parking lot. Forgive me, Father, but my eyes are glued to the sway of her ample behind in black and white pinstriped pants. She has a nice, slim-thick figure. She made it seem like I'm a youngin' when it looks like we're the same age of thirty-three. Even if she's older, I'm not scared. She's the first woman in years that's garnered my attention. And in one glance.

She's physically beautiful, no doubt, with her brown skin, big expressive eyes, full lips and coily hair. But something internally has me drawn like a moth to a flame. Her vibe, aura, spirit, hooked my attention without my consent.

I know my mom picked up on it too. Just this morning, she was praying *again* for me to find my Ruth, not necessarily saying Tanya is her. My family knows I prefer not to be alone when talking to women in the congregation. Unfortunately, pastors sometimes get a bad rap for scandals in the church. But from my experience, women hound on pastors with no decorum, respect or shame—whether the man of God is married or not. I'm single and have been for eight years.

My high school sweetheart, Sasha, and I married a year after we graduated. We were so in love, nobody could tell us anything. We had big plans. I would work at my family-owned, small car dealership to help it grow while I attended Bible College to one day become a prominent pastor. Sasha would attend college to get her nursing degree to become a nurse practitioner. We had twins when we turned twenty-three. A boy, Ace, and daughter, A'Mya.

We were struggling financially, living in a one-bedroom apartment, but we had love and each other. I thought we were all good until a year later, Sasha left me and filed for divorce. Apparently, my dreams for success weren't happening fast enough. Her leaving broke something in me. I was bitter for a long time. After all these years, I'm sometimes still affected by it. She remarried nine months after the divorce was final to an older man whose wife had died from cancer. He's a mega church pastor with over 10,000 members in Landover, Maryland.

"Daddy, can we go to Panera for lunch?" A'Mya, my ten-year-old daughter, asks with Ace and my mom right behind her.

"Sure, baby. We can stop at Panera, then go straight home because you both have to finish your essays for English."

I have full custody of the twins. Surprisingly, Sasha didn't put up much of a fight. She got pregnant a couple months after remarrying, which worked to my advantage. Sasha felt it would be best if I had full custody for her to adjust to being a newlywed, first lady of a megachurch and having a new baby on the way. God worked that out because I don't know how I would've handled not being with my children the majority of the time.

Sasha now has three children with her husband. The twins are with her biweekly, Thursday to Sunday. I don't receive child support from her, although I'm entitled to. She covers half of their school tuition and does her part financially when they're with her.

"I'm almost done with mine. I don't know about A'Mya," Ace informs me.

"Did Miss Tanya leave already?" Mom asks, looking over my shoulder.

"Not so subtle, Ma," I tease her.

She feigns innocence. "What do you mean? I thought she was nice."

"Yeah, and I know what else you're thinking."

She throws her hand on her hip. "Humph! Don't say I've never tried to hook you up."

"I don't need your help, Ma." I walk over to lock the doors of the church. With only 288 members, including children, and one 9 a.m. Sunday service, everyone is mostly gone for the day since there are no after service events this Sunday. I know many churches have more than one Sunday service, but that requires too much time, effort and money, trying to accommodate everyone when someone still won't be satisfied. My motto is, either people are going to show up or they won't. Perhaps that's why House of Praise only has close to 300 members. Regardless, I'm doing things the way the Lord sees fit.

"This is good, and it is pleasing in the sight of God our Savior." 1 Timothy 2:3. Pastoring a megachurch used to be my dream, but God has blessed me with contentment right where I am. It took years to grow the church to what it is today. For me, this is my megachurch.

"I know you don't. The women in the church act like they're in heat when you're around." She walks behind me, so the twins don't hear her. "I felt something good about her in my spirit the second I laid eyes on her. She's going to be my daughter-in-law."

"Ma!"

"What? Now you know I don't go around claiming anyone as such. Trust that I know what I'm saying."

"Who's to say she'll even come back to the church?"

"Did you say something to turn her off?" Ma asks, almost indignant. I wanna laugh at the dumbfounded look on her face.

"No, I didn't… Where is your husband?" I'm not interested in discussing the mirage of feelings I have about meeting Tanya a few short moments ago. It could all be nothing really. Just passing feelings in a brief moment of time.

"Boy!" She playfully swats me on the arm. "Your daddy is locking up. Now what did you say to Tanya?"

"Nothing, Ma. She said she will be at the new members' class."

"Hmm. Well, I will also be looking out for her next Sunday."

"Ma, please. If what you feel is true, let it happen organically. All things happen in due season. Me finding my Ruth will as well."

Ma smiles brightly, then steps closer to pat my beard covered cheeks. "You're right, son. I won't interfere."

"Thank you."

We all spend the next few minutes locking doors and securing the grounds. The church is only big enough to hold three hundred people in the sanctuary with six classrooms and a church office. It's all fully owned by me. No loan.

My ownership in the family dealership helped. Over the years, the family business has gone from selling only older model, used cars to becoming a Ford Dealership. We now sell and lease brand new cars as well. God has blessed me and my dad tremendously with our business. I know my grandfather would be proud. He passed down the business to my dad and my dad passed it on to me. I plan on passing it down to Ace and A'Mya, if they want it.

I don't take home a salary from the church. All the tithes and offerings go to the small staff, maintaining the church, and back into the community.

I'm so glad God got me off the wrong path I was on in my teens. Even though I had a stable home with both parents, I was for the streets. I kept getting into all kinds of problems for no good reason other than trying to keep up with the crowd. It took me almost going to jail for false identity for a gas station robbery before I finally got on the straight and narrow. I really found Jesus then.

As the twins and I load into my brand-new Ford Expedition, my thoughts travel back to Tanya. I'm already looking forward to seeing her next Sunday.

3
TANYA

"Girl, you have the rich auntie vibe something serious," my best and only friend besides my mama, Janet, says after I approach the table at the diner.

I remove my oversized, designer shades from covering my eyes as I take a seat. Besides my purse, it's the only designer I'm flaunting. I'm wealthy, but I was never into wearing big brand labels. Don't get me wrong, I stay looking fly, but on a budget.

"I was taught by the best."

Janet is five years older than me. We met over ten years ago when we both worked for the federal government. We're both childless and husbandless. However, she's enjoyed being a cougar with her boy toy, Carlos, for the past year.

"That you have. And you're alive, which means hell doesn't want you yet for lusting over your pastor." Janet giggles.

I throw the paper napkin on my plate at her, which makes her laugh harder.

"Shut up! It's not my fault God made him so fine. But I'm not going to overstep. For one, he's my pastor. For two, he's too young. You may be comfortable dating younger men, but I'm not."

"Honey, I'm not just dating them, I'm getting the best ride of my life..." Janet twerks in her seat.

I shake my head with a smile. Janet believes in God and respects my renewed walk of faith, but it's not the journey she's on now.

"I understand your point though. Dating a pastor, regardless, could be tricky. Because it's like you're not just dating the man, you're dating the whole church with their expectations."

"Well, it's not my problem because Pastor Antwain is strictly just my pastor."

"Hmm. I'm going to church with you next Sunday to see him for myself. You've hyped this man up so much, I've got to see if he's real."

"Oh, he's real and you better not start fantasizing about him either." I'm dead serious, which shocks me.

Janet gives me a knowing look. "Girl, you've got it bad. Lord, please help my friend. I don't want her to go to hell."

A waiter comes over to take our breakfast orders.

"Did you see the report for this month?" Janet asks after the waiter leaves.

"Yeah. Profits are great."

After years of working as Human Resource executives, six years ago, Janet and I created a platform, HireRight, to help companies post job listings and keep track of resumes, interviews, follow ups, and onboarding of staff. Three years ago, we sold the platform for ten million each and we continue to receive decent percentage of profits. We receive monthly and quarterly reports to stay abreast of our brainchild. Whenever they need our insight on anything, we charge them a consultant fee.

Some people believe we shouldn't have sold HireRight, but neither me nor Janet wanted to deal with the stress of running the business. Plus, we have no children to pass it down to.

"Hi, Tanya."

I look up to find Mrs. Hall and Antwain's sister standing at our table.

I move to stand. "Hi, Mrs. Hall –"

"No, no. Stay seated, dear. I noticed you on the way to our table and just wanted to say hi. This is my daughter, Alicia. She and her hubby played hooky from church yesterday."

It's hard to tell Alicia's age, but I do recall hearing that she's Antwain's older sister. Maybe she's in her late thirties. Black don't crack though, because she looks like she's in her late twenties.

"Ma!" Alicia says in mock shame. "Hi, Tanya. You must have left a mark on my mother because she mentioned you to me when I picked her up for breakfast. Now here you are. It's nice to meet you."

Wow. Did I leave that good of an impression in such a short time?

"We only met briefly. It's nice to meet you, Alicia. This is my best friend, Janet."

"Good morning, Mrs. Hall and Alicia," Janet greets them.

"Good morning," they respond in unison.

"We'll leave you be. I hope to see you at church next Sunday," Mrs. Hall says before walking off.

"I'll be there. Enjoy your breakfast."

I turn back to find Janet staring at me in wonderment. "You in there now, Tanya. If his mama likes you, it's a wrap. You gon' be first lady real soon."

"Shut up!" I laugh. I'm both intrigued and scared out of my mind.

Pastor Antwain is just my pastor. Nothing more, nothing less.

4
ANTWAIN

"Oh snap! My boy pulled out the Armani suit for today. And is that Stefano Ricci, Royal Eagle cologne I smell? My man, which one of them ladies in the church snag your attention?" My boy from fifth grade, Ezra, leans against my desk.

I'm standing in front of a mirror in my office, fixing my necktie. Service starts in thirty minutes. I'm only here three days a week—Sundays, Wednesdays and Thursdays. The other days I dedicate to the dealership.

My thoughts quickly go to Tanya. I had her in mind when I got dressed this morning. She has snuck herself into my psyche all week. That alone lets me know I need to get to know her on a personal level. Yet I have no clue how to do it.

Since my divorce, I haven't given women much attention. Only a handful of times, temptation got the best of me when I needed to relieve stress the first couple of years after Sasha left. I've been completely celibate the last six years, especially when I started the church. I haven't been on a date in ages. And I certainly have never entertained a woman in my congregation.

I shouldn't even be considering Tanya, but my expensive attire and cologne for the day says otherwise. I want to impress her. I haven't wanted to impress a woman since Sasha – the woman who trampled over my heart with no remorse.

"There's someone. But it may be all in my head. It doesn't help that Ma instantly took a liking to her, calling her her future daughter-in-law."

"Word? Ma co-signed?"

"Word. I don't even know if she's coming to church today. If she does, I don't know how to approach her in that way. How do I go from Pastor Antwain, to 'yo shawty let me take you out'?"

Ezra bends over laughing at my expense. Easy for him. He's been married for five years.

"Nigga, I know you ain't over there laughing when I'm serious. Help ya boy out." I'm a man of God, but I'm not far removed from where I come from.

Ezra sits upright, patting his chest like he's recovering from the best joke of his life. I'm starting to reevaluate our friendship. This fool really taking me for jokes when I need advice.

I turn away from the mirror, mean-mugging him. "Are you done?"

"Yeah...Yeah." He wipes tears from his eyes. "I know it's been a while, but you still that dude. It's like riding a bike. Be straight up with your intentions, then let things fall as they may. Either she's down or she's not."

Simple, but it will have to work. "Yeah, you're right."

I just hope I don't punk up.

"Your message blessed me today, Pastor Antwain." Sister Eva and Brother Charles greet me in the church foyer. They are probably the hundredth persons I've spoken to in the past twenty minutes, and I have yet to see Tanya walk by.

I know she attended service today. I felt it when she walked into the sanctuary. I was already seated up front right before the choir took the stage. I looked over my shoulder, and she and another woman walked in together. I followed her with my eyes all the way to their seats. Left section, tenth row.

"I'm happy you were blessed. Now it's your duty to take heed of God's message," I reply distractedly, looking over their shoulders for *her*.

"Will do pastor. See you next Sunday." The couple walks away.

Ezra is standing next to me today because he wants to witness me fumble with Tanya. It seems I may not get a chance to.

Where is she?

That's when I see her walking out the sanctuary talking with Alicia. When did they become aquatinted?

"That must be her," Ezra notices who's captured my attention. "The one in the yellow or red?"

"Yellow." *It sure looks good on her.*

"Oh dawg, I see why you were having a mini meltdown. She badder than a mutha."

"Yeah. But it's more than her outer beauty that's got me stuck."

1 Peter 3:3-4 enters my thoughts. "*Your beauty should not come from outward adornment, such as elaborate hairstyles and the wearing of gold jewelry or fine clothes. Rather, it should be that of your inner self, the unfading beauty of a gentle and quiet spirit, which is of great worth in God's sight.*"

Tanya and her friend end their talk with Alicia, then turn their attention towards me and Ezra. I can sense Tanya's apprehension. Is she as affected as I am? Or maybe she's just not that into me.

"Now or never," Ezra says as they approach us.

My heart gallops as I watch Tanya drawing near in her flowy, yellow, knee-high dress. She's effortlessly gorgeous. I bite my lip in admiration. I would prefer biting hers.

Down boy! He hasn't been excited in a long while.

"Good day, Pastor Antwain. This is my friend, Janet."

"Good day, Tanya." My eyes are locked on hers. "Nice to meet you, Janet. Thanks for attending service today. Tanya, Janet, this is my friend, Ezra." My eyes never leave hers. I don't pay much attention to Ezra greeting the ladies.

"Pastor Antwain, you've certainly lived up to the legend," Janet says.

I finally look at her. She's a good-looking woman. "Has Tanya talked about me?" Curiosity gets the best of me.

"She hasn't stopped," Janet freely admits. I like her.

"Really, Janet?!" Tanya looks embarrassed. She shouldn't be.

Ezra chuckles.

I take Tanya's hand, gently pulling her away from our friends. "Can I take you out on a date?" I quickly ask before I lose my nerve. I flash a smile for good measure.

"A date? Pastor An –"

"Antwain, please. I'm not trying to be your pastor right now."

I see a flash of desire in her eyes, then too quickly, it's gone.

"I – I don't think that's a good idea. I'm too old for you."

"Let me be the judge of that. How old are you?"

"Forty-five."

I do quick math in my head. She's twelve years older than me and I couldn't care less. "I see no problem."

She's shocked. "You don't?"

I shake my head. "No. Do you?"

"No... yes!"

"I believed you the first time. So, a date? Tomorrow at six?"

"O – kay."

I pull my cellphone from my suit jacket pocket. "Key in your number, please."

Tanya takes my phone to add her number then hands it back to me.

"Are you allergic to anything?" I ask while fighting with everything in me not to kiss the soul from her body. We might as well be the only two in this building because only she and I exist in my mind right now.

"No."

"I will call you about the details of our date this evening. Anticipate my call."

"I already am." She looks like she can't believe she said that out loud.

I'm just happy to know we're both feeling each other.

5
ANTWAIN

I leave church on cloud nine. Tanya said yes to a date. Now I need to figure out where I'm going to take her. I've been wracking my brain since trying to figure out what we can do on our first date. I keep drawing back to a classic – dinner and a movie.

I enjoy the quiet of my 3500-square-foot home when I enter through the garage into the top-of-the-line kitchen. The twins are with their mother until this evening. This is the type of home Sasha and I had dreams of when we got married at nineteen years old. She didn't give me a chance to fulfill it with her.

I hated Sasha for a long time after she left. It's only because of my faith that I was able to let the anger go and forgive her. She's still not my favorite person in the world. I will always have love for her though as the mother of my children.

I throw my keys on the granite countertop before washing my hands then making a beeline to the fridge. Ma always cooks huge meals Saturday evenings, cooking enough for her household, mine, and Alicia's. I pull out the food containers to fix my plate.

While eating, I search on my cellphone for movie listings. Then I pinpoint a place for dinner. Confident with my plans, I decide to call Tanya.

She answers on the second ring. "Hello, Antwain?"

"Are you expecting someone else?" Mostly done with my food, I push it aside on the countertop.

"No, just you."

"Hmm, I like the sound of that."

Tanya laughs which makes me smile. "So, what are our date plans?"

"I decided to keep it simple. Dinner and a movie." I look out my large kitchen window into my wide backyard. I need to plant some spring flowers.

"I'm a simple woman, which makes that perfect."

"Cool. We'll have Indian food for dinner then walk over to the AMC for the movie. Can I pick you up?"

"No offense, Pastor Antwain, but you're still a guy I don't know. I don't invite strangers to my home."

I chuckle. "None taken. The gentleman in me had to ask."

"I appreciate that. Besides, I want to drive in case I need to bounce if our date is lame."

"Oh really?"

"Yes, really. But I have a feeling that won't be the case."

My phone chimes with an incoming call. It's A'Mya calling me from her iPad since I haven't given her and Ace cellphones yet.

"Tanya, I would love to finish this conversation, but my baby girl is calling. Can I call you back later?"

"Sure, no problem. Talk to you later, Antwain."

I love the way she says my name.

"Thanks. Later, Tanya."

I end her call, then answer A'Mya's.

"Da – daddy!" She's crying which immediately puts me in beast mode.

I stand from the kitchen stool. "What's the matter, baby? Why are you crying?"

"MmmMr. Frederick gave me and Ace a spppanking –"

"What?"

Oh no! That muthaf – that nigga did not put his hands on my kids. I grab my keys off the counter. Over the years, me and Sasha's new husband have had few words for each other. I let him know from day one, big time Pastor or not, he was not to play when it came to my children. Things had been kosher with us since.

Not today!

I head for my Ford Mustang in the garage. "Tell me everything that happened, baby. I'm on my way."

A'Mya sniffles and it's taking everything in me to remain calm. Yes, I discipline my kids and Sasha does too. Yes, they cry and have meltdowns when they don't get their way, typical childhood behavior, but the twins are good kids. They are being raised well, despite not having both parents in the same home. Frederick, however, and anyone who isn't the twins' *biological* parent, are not allowed to use corporal punishment on my children. Ever!

"Fendi was running around..." she says, referring to her seven-year-old stepsister. "...And me and Ace was telling her stop because we know that mommy and Mr. Frederick don't like running in the house. She kept running and knocked over a big pretty vase. Me and Ace was helping her clean it up when Mr. Frederick came in the living room, started yelling at us. Fendi lied and said me and Ace did it. That's when he spanked me and Ace on the butts with his hand."

Oh, you like using your hands muthaf – Lord, oh Lord, help me because I'm about to whoop his ass.

Do not be quick in spirit to be angry. For anger is in the heart of fools. Ecclesiastes 7:9

The Scripture eases my anger only slightly as I zoom out of my driveway. "All right, baby girl, you won't have to worry about him spanking you again. Where's Ace?"

"He's packing our stuff. I told him I was calling you."

My son knows what's up. They are coming home with me when I get there. Forget the few more hours they have with their mom. Speaking of which, "Where's your mother?"

"She should be here soon. There was a women's ministry meeting at church."

"All right, I'll be there in fifteen minutes. Stay on the phone with me."

Thirteen minutes later, I speed up the long driveway of the Henderson residence. I end the call with A'Mya. Sasha's red Tesla is in the driveway. Good. My car is barely in park while I'm hopping out. I jog up the stairs to the massive, mahogany, double front doors, and bang on the door.

Seconds later, Sasha is answering the door, still dressed to kill in her Sunday best. "Why are you banging on the door like you're the police? And why are you here? I drop the twins off at six." She has scowl on her perfectly made-up face. My attraction to her died the instant I came home eight years ago and she was gone. I had loved this woman fiercely. I would've done anything to make her happy. No more.

"Where ya husband at?" In this moment, all my years of Bible College move out the way and enters Antwain from the block.

"Daddy!" A'Mya yells, coming down the spiral staircase from the bedrooms with Ace tugging their book bags behind him.

"Hey, baby." I step inside the over-the-top foyer of their million-dollar home. Sasha side eyes me as I wait for the twins to come near. "Go wait in the car." I kiss both A'Mya and Ace on the forehead.

"Bye, mommy," the twins say in unison before giving her a hug.

I wait until they're out of earshot before addressing Sasha again. "Go get Frederick."

"What is this about, Antwain?" She folds her arms across her chest.

"Your husband putting his hands on my kids. Now go get homeboy." My fingers flex at my sides.

"He did what?!"

That's right, she wasn't here. "Frederick spanked our twins because Fendi lied and said they were running in the house and broke a vase." It's no question that A'Mya was telling the truth. She knows the consequences of lying to me.

"Are you sure it wasn't a tap?"

I look at Sasha like she has roaches crawling out her nostrils. "Our daughter called me crying because he put his hands on her. I have no problem with my children being disciplined when necessary, but he crossed the line big time when he spanked them."

"I wasn't here. I just got in from a church meeting. Let me talk to him. I promise it will never happen again."

"You're right about that. And I'll be the one to let him know." I look over her shoulder. "Yo, Freddy! Bring your punk a –"

"Antwain! Enough. You're a pastor and you're here acting like a gutta ghetto thug. Haven't you passed that stage in your life?"

"Not when it pertains to my kids. The Bible says there's a time for love and a time for war. It's war time. Tell him to come before I find him!"

"Not until you calm down." Sasha puts her palm against my chest in an attempt to stop me from moving forward.

"What is all this ruckus?" Freddy Krueger asks, coming from the east side of their home. His footsteps echo on the marble floors. He's sixty and looks like a corpse. Sasha had to have married him for his money. Thankfully, their kids got her genes.

I step toward him despite Sasha tugging on my arm. She knows how I got down back in the day. I hit Frederick with a right hook before he knows what's happening. He falls flat on his behind, holding his jaw. Sasha screams, going to his aid.

"Don't you ever in your life touch my children again! You're only being spared because of my faith. I won't be so forgiving if I have to address this situation

again." I turn on my heels and head out.

Geriatric looking, Viagra popping fool.

6
TANYA

I shouldn't have agreed to this date with Antwain, but I did. The man is hard to resist. But he's way too young for me. I've never dated anyone more than five years younger than me. What could we possibly have in common? If I was still out here living outside the will of God, sex would most definitely be on the table – that *would* make us compatible.

It's not. I'm saved and celibate. And he's a pastor, for goodness sake. So, with sex not being an option, why waste both our times with a date that won't lead anywhere? I'm ready to find a good man to settle down with. I don't have interest in meaningless relationships. Been there, done that.

I'm not the woman someone young as Antwain would seek for a wife. If he wants more kids, I'm not it. Besides not being physically able to carry babies, I'm knocking on menopause's door. He says he's cool with our twelve years difference. I doubt that will remain.

All this runs through my mind in a loop as I drive to meet Antwain at the entertainment plaza in Alexandria, Virginia for our date. I'm not going to front—despite my reservations, I'm excited. Something must be wrong with me. I'm either hot or cold regarding this man.

I find a perfect parking spot right next to Antwain's blue Mustang. He had called me when he pulled up, letting me know where he was parked in the lot. He's leaning against the hood of his car looking like a model as I reverse into the available spot. He's at my driver's side door as soon I shift the gear to my Range Rover into park.

"Good evening, gorgeous." He opens my car door for me, handing me a vase filled with bright colored flowers that smell so good. I hadn't noticed him holding the vase when I pulled up.

"Thank you! These are beautiful. You're starting our date off right."

"I aim to please." Antwain blesses me with his smile.

I take a deep whiff of the flowers before leaning over to place the vase in the passenger seat.

"Can I have a hug?" he asks after helping me out of my vehicle.

"Yeah, sure –"

Antwain's strong arms encircle me, which instantly send the walls I've erected over the years tumbling down. I didn't know I needed a hug this badly. From *him*. I almost tear up when, too soon, he's stepping out of our embrace.

Moments later, we're walking towards the Indian restaurant for dinner. Antwain surprises me by taking my hand in his.

"I hope you don't mind." He looks over at me.

I absolutely do not mind.

"No, it's fine." I smile up at him.

I've had sex with seven men in the course of my life, dated many more, yet Antwain is one of three whom I've shared this type of intimacy with. That fact screams loudly in my soul. How is it that we can give our bodies so freely, yet withhold the vulnerable parts of us?

"We are not withholding our affection from you, but you are withholding yours from us." 2 Corinthians 6:12. Wow, I think about the Scripture Holy Spirit brings to my memory. *Being vulnerable is no easy feat.*

****

"Wait a minute, you punched him?" My mouth hangs open in shock. Pastor has a bad-boy side?

"Yeah, not one of my finer moments. The Lord chastised me for it too. I should have handled it better. But I felt justified. Nobody messes with my kids. He called me later that evening to apologize for overstepping and I apologized too. Fendi also apologized to the twins for lying."

It's getting hot in here. I reach for my glass of water, bypassing my glass of wine; I take a big gulp. Hearing Antwain talk about the incident yesterday defending his kids heightens my attraction for him. Like it's not to the moon already.

"Honestly, I would feel the same way too."

"Yeah? You have kids?"

I almost choke. I swallow, then catch my breath, placing the glass of water on the table next to my plate of butter chicken and rice. Now is when he'll be making the quickest exit.

"I don't have kids." I look across the table at him.

"You don't want any, or just never found the right guy to have them with?" He reaches for his own glass of water for a sip.

"I wanted kids. I just couldn't have them."

I watch his body language for any signs of disappointment. He gives me nothing. His face is blank of emotions.

"Sorry. How have you dealt with that over the years?"

"I…I've grown to accept it. It was extremely hard at first. Sometimes, I wished I never got an abortion at sixteen –"

No I didn't just freely put my business out there. I'm not ashamed of it because I've been redeemed. I just don't do this. Especially on a first date.

"Tanya, I want to know all of you. You can talk to me about any and everything. Anytime. Continue, please."

Okay cub, you really about to bring the cougar out in me.

"After finding out that the illegal abortion I had contributed to me not being able to carry children, I went into a mini depression for a few months. To this day, my parents know nothing about me having an abortion as a teenager. My father never will because he died a few years ago. I'm in a much better place now though. Being childless afforded me the opportunity to travel the world, which also helped me overcome my depression."

"I'm happy you're in a good place in your life with that…Would you be interested in adopting or being a stepparent?"

I see what he did there. My lips curl up in a smile as I watch him eat.

"Adoption no. Stepmom, I'm definitely open to it. I just have to find the right man with the perfect kids," I tease.

"Look no further, baby." Antwain wiggles his eyebrows.

I laugh out loud. This man. *Lord, why did you make him so young?*

"Antwain, I'm enjoying our date so far, but let's be real. I'm too old for you. I've never dated someone so much younger."

I know I sound like a broken record, but if I were to set aside my concerns about being older, fall for him – which I know will be easy – and he decides later this isn't for him, I will be crushed. I'm seriously trying to protect my heart and his.

I pick up my glass of wine to take a big gulp.

"Tanya, I don't make a habit of saying things I don't mean. I don't care that you are twelve years older than me. But if you do, then we can end the date here and become friends. I want more than that though and I'm hoping you do too."

"Why?"

"Why you?" he asks.

I nod.

"When I laid eyes on you, my spirit said, *she's the one*. Which is something I didn't even get with my ex-wife."

Antwain says it with such assurance that I have no choice but to believe him. He's not spitting game. I've encountered enough men to know the difference. A man knows what he wants, whether he chooses to act on it or not.

I swallow the lump that formed in my throat. This thing between us is getting heavy – fast. Which makes me nervous for reasons beyond our age difference.

I don't want to mess this up.

"Let's see how the rest of this dates goes, then I'll give you my answer."

"Bet," he says with a wink.

✱✱✱

"Did you enjoy the movie?" I ask as we walk out of the theatre into the night, holding hands.

"I did. I enjoyed your company even more."

"You and these smooth lines. This date has definitely put you in a different light for me. You're one cool pastor, Antwain. I admire the fact that even though you preach from the pulpit, you're still true to who you are and where you came from. I'm digging the bad-boy swag. You don't try to act holyfied."

He gives my hand a gentle squeeze while we maneuver through the crowd walking along the sidewalk toward the parking lot. "All I know how to be is me. That's what the Lord requires of me. Unfortunately, many Christians fall into the trap of thinking they have to act saved. Christianity isn't an act; it's a lifestyle."

"It is. I lost my way when I turned thirty. I'm back now. I thank God He didn't give up on me. Interestingly, I remember most of the Scriptures I memorized way back then. The Bible is true – *"Direct your children onto the right path, and when they are older, they will not leave it."*

"Proverbs twenty-two verse six."

"Yup!"

"Was there anything in particular that made you come back to the faith?" Antwain asks as we cross over to the expansive parking lot.

"Life, dating, and Holy Spirit telling me to bring my butt home." I laugh. Antwain does too.

"I'm happy you obeyed. Otherwise, you would've had me still praying to find my Ruth. You had me struggling out here for years, woman."

Laughter bubbles from my lips. "You're silly."

"Nah. I'm dead serious. Ya boy been out here bad, Tanya. You had my mom bruising her knees every time she knelt to pray for you." Antwain grins.

"Well, I'm here now."

"To stay, I hope?" he asks with seriousness as we stop in front of my car.

"For as long as you'll have me." I bite down on my lip as I stare up at him.

Antwain steps closer, forcing me to lean against the driver's side door of my Range Rover. The chemistry between us as been astronomical since the first time we stood in front of each other.

He lifts his hand to cup my cheek. I inhale deeply in anticipation.

Please, please, please kiss me.

Antwain swipes his thumb across my bottom lip. My tongue eagerly swipes out to lick his finger like a fiend. I should be ashamed by my desperateness, but heck I'm over forty, so I'm not. I want this man something serious. Even if all I can indulge in is a kiss.

Antwain crashes his firm, delicious lips against mine and my legs buckle from the overwhelming feeling of relief of finally experiencing this moment. Antwain stops my fall by placing his hand against my waist. My arms snake around his neck, pulling him closer. When he swipes his tongue into my mouth, I moan loudly. Kissing never felt so good.

All too soon, Antwain is slowly separating his lips from mine. "We better stop before we get into something we ain't got no business getting into." He takes a step back from me. I avert my eyes from his hard to miss attraction.

"Yeah. W…we should leave." I press my key fob to unlock my car.

"Let's be clear—you're mine now and I'm all yours," he asserts, which doesn't help to subside my arousal.

"Oh, you got that right. You can't kiss me like that and expect me to walk away easily."

He grins wickedly while opening my car door for me. "I'll follow you home to make sure you arrive safely."

"Okay. Don't get any ideas about coming in for nightcap," I tease.

Antwain groans. "I'mma need Jesus to come down from heaven to help me survive dating you," he jokes.

Yeah, me too.

7
ANTWAIN

"You got some pep in your step this morning. Is it that young lady your mom told me about?"

"What are you doing here, old man?" I joke to my dad as I enter the executive office for the dealership. "You're practically retired."

My dad looks like an older version of me. He's sixty-eight, but looks way younger.

"I'll retire when I'm dead!" he exclaims adamantly. He takes a sip from his coffee cup. He's sitting in one of the visitor's seats in my large, professionally decorated office.

I take a seat behind my desk.

"So, who's got you smiling so hard?" Dad continues probing.

I've been thinking about my date last night with Tanya since I got up this morning. Heck, I even dreamt about it. Miss Freeman got me sprung and it's only been one date. We're dating exclusively now which means there will be more opportunity to get to know each other better.

"Tanya Freeman. We're officially a couple." I lean against my comfortable swivel chair.

"So your mama was right. She's your future wife?"

"It's early. But I really think so, Dad."

"Then I look forward to meeting her. You know I always thought you and Sasha married too soon, being babies fresh out of high school. You're older and more mature, a great dad, businessman and pastor. I know you're ready to be a husband again. And the next time will be forever."

"Thanks, Dad." What he said means a lot. I'm not too old to appreciate my father's blessing.

"Invite her over to our house for dinner on Saturday. Something tells me y'all ain't gon' be courting soon before you put a ring on it." He laughs boisterously. "I admire you single Christian folks abstaining from sex, but the good Lord knows why He kept me married for almost forty years. I be needing to get my thang wet often."

My ears start to bleed. "Naw, Pops! I don't need to be hearing all that. You talking 'bout my mama, man." I have a scowl on my face in disgust.

My old man leans forward laughing, slapping his knee.

"I will ask Tanya about dinner. I don't want to introduce her to the twins yet. Although I'm sure about wanting to fully pursue a relationship with her, I want to get to know her more first."

"Smart move. Does she have kids?"

I shake my head. "She doesn't. She doesn't mind being a stepmom one day either." Tanya not being able to have children doesn't bother me. I have the perfect pair of children. I never thought of having more, especially after the disastrous way my marriage ended.

"All right. What does she do for a living?"

"She's retired –"

"Retired? Son, how old is this woman?" Dad sits ramrod straight, shooting daggers at me.

I bite back a laugh. "She's not old like you, so chill. She's a retired human resource executive and she and her best friend sold a program they created a few years ago for quite a bit of money. Tanya is twelve years older than me."

He clutches his chest. "Oh, thank God!" he exclaims dramatically. I laugh at him. "I know women being cougars are a thing, but it would've have been strange seeing my son date a woman close to my age."

"Yeah."

"Your mom and sister like her based on the conversation I overheard them having. Have you told them you and Tanya are dating?"

I shake my head. "Nah. We just made things official last night."

"Then wait until dinner on Saturday to say anything. For once, I'll have one up on them." He sips his coffee.

I pull my cellphone from my pocket to send Tanya a text. We've already spoken to each other on my way to the office this morning.

Antwain: Hey, my dad invited you for dinner this Saturday. Are you available?

I place my cellphone on the desk as Dad and I's conversation moves to business. Short minutes later, Tanya replies.

Tanya: Wow, introducing me to the family as your woman already? Sure, I would love to.

Antwain: Or I can get a billboard to announce to everyone traveling on I-95.

Tanya: LOL. I don't care about everyone else. I look forward to dinner on Saturday and our lunch date later today.

Antwain: Me too. See you later Cougar.

I laugh to myself, teasing her.

Tanya: You better behave Cub. See you soon.

"She looks good on you, son. Real good," Dad says, pulling my attention back to him.

"Yeah, she does."

8
TANYA

It's mid June. Three months since Antwain and I became a couple. Whether it's too soon or not – I'm in love with that man. He's the epitome of a good man. Our personalities gel well with each other's. We've even had a couple disagreements over petty things that we handled well.

I'd been in love once before with Jackson Dean when I was twenty-seven. We met on a five-hour flight from Vegas back to DC. We dated for almost two years. I thought he would pop the question, but I found out he had a wife and three boys when I saw them as a family at a restaurant. They were celebrating their eldest son's thirteenth birthday.

I showed my butt off that night. The situation pulled me all the way out of character because at that time, I was heavy in my Christian faith before I gave up on it a couple years later. I was cussing, throwing food, plates, drinks, *everythang* at Jackson and his trifling behind. I didn't care that I was making a fool of myself. He hurt me to the core. Blindsided me in the worst way. Two men from security had to drag me out of the upscale restaurant, kicking and screaming. I'm probably still banned to this day.

And that lowdown dirty hyena had the audacity to come to my home, begging for forgiveness. I had regained my common sense by then because otherwise, I would've ended up in jail for the bodily harm I would've inflicted on him. I didn't bother opening my door as he wore the doorbell out. I called the cops and had them deal with removing him from my property.

His wife divorced him, taking him for everything she could in the settlement. I have no idea what's become of his life.

This love I feel for Antwain is much different. It's beyond anything I felt for Jackson. I haven't told him how I feel yet 'cause I find myself still trying to play it safe when I really want to move at lightning speed.

"Hey," Alicia says when she notices me in the doorway of one of the Sunday school classrooms. Church let out about twenty minutes ago.

"Hey, girl. Need help?" I walk further into the room, placing my purse on one of the desks before walking closer to help her pack supplies into a cabinet.

"Thanks…Antwain told me you're interested in volunteering to teach the second and third grade class."

"Yeah, I think I can handle a bunch of seven and eight-year-olds. Antwain said the combined classes have nine kids?"

We continue putting the pencils, pens, papers, Bibles, etcetera away in the cabinet.

"Yup. Nine students. You will only need to volunteer the second and fourth Sunday of the month. The teacher we had before is no longer able to do it, which is why I've stepped in to help until we find a replacement. There's a curriculum we use that's already preset for the year, so no need to worry about creating a lesson." Alicia works part time as the church secretary, along with running a candle-making business that keeps her plenty busy.

"Perfect! I can handle that." Now that I'm a member of the church, I've felt Holy Spirit urging me to volunteer my time in ministry. I'm happy to help.

Alicia closes then locks the cabinet. "Awesome. Thanks, Tanya. I will add you to the schedule." She walks over to the teacher's desk, picking up a large book. "This is your copy of the lesson plans."

I accept the book from her. We chat for a few more minutes before she has to leave.

"Anyway, Sis, hubby and the teens are waiting for me in the car. I'll call you later this week." Alicia and I hug before walking out the classroom. She heads left and I head right toward the church office to touch base with Antwain before I leave to go to my mom's house.

I look in my purse for my cellphone that's dinging from a text message alert. I retrieve it, reading a message from my mom asking me if Antwain wants her to make him another peach pie. I immediately text yes because I know what his answer will be.

He and my mom hit it off instantly the first time they met. It was the Sunday after I had dinner at his parents' home, meeting his dad officially for the first time. I haven't been introduced to the twins yet and I respect Antwain's stance on waiting.

My mom loves her some Antwain. She treats him like the son she always wanted. I love it! Because if things between Antwain and I continue to go as great as they are, I hope he will be her son for real. By marriage.

"Ahhh!" I yelp when someone bumps against my arm. Hard. I look up from my phone. Corine is standing in front of me with a stank look on her face. "Sorry would be nice!" I snap. I squeeze my cellphone in my hand to stop the urge to strike her. Her hostile vibe got me jacked up. If she thinks I won't drag her in this church…

What is her problem?

"You stop messing with my man would be nice," she enunciates each word while rolling her neck.

"Your man?" I raise my brow.

"Don't act stupid, Ms. Thang. I see you being chummy with Pastor Antwain. He's mine. He was at my house all last night as a matter of fact." Her red lips form into a smirk.

Interesting. Antwain and I drove back from Luray Caverns yesterday evening after spending the whole day in Virginia. After he dropped me home, we spoke on the phone until close to midnight because we both had to get up early for church today.

I play along with her charade to see how delusional she is. "Oh, really?" I look over her shoulder. "Dad!" I call out to Mr. Hall. He just stepped out of the men's room a few feet away.

"Hey, Tanya. You're here late," he approaches us.

When Corine sees who it is, her eyes widen.

"Yeah, I was on my way to the office when this young lady stopped me to inform me that she's Pastor Antwain's woman. Are you aware of their relationship?"

Mr. Hall looks at Corine with disdain. "Sister Corine, not only are you lying in the house of the Lord, but on your man of God. Have you no shame?"

"I – I... she misunderstood what I –"

This woman really needs Jesus. "I didn't misunderstand you saying, *'he's mine and was at my house all last night.'*" I repeat her words back to her.

Mr. Hall shakes his head disapprovingly. "This isn't the first time you've been caught in a lie about a gentleman in this church. I'm sure the church board would agree it's grounds for you not to return."

"What?! Over some she say, she say? I don't want to find another church," Corine whines like a spoiled brat.

"We can't have you creating discord either. Please leave!" Mr. Hall points to the exit.

"Umph! This ain't the only church with fine men in it." She turns around and sashays away.

Wow! I see what Antwain meant about people causing drama and scandal in the church.

9
ANTWAIN

"Daddy, can Fendi sleep over at our house on Friday?" A'Mya asks for the umpteenth time since Sasha dropped them off early at the church. This is Sasha's weekend, but she and Frederick are heading out of town for a conference he's speaking at on Tuesday.

"I don't know, A'Mya. I will talk to your mom about it." Even though Fendi and A'Mya have a three-year age difference, they have become the best of friends since that incident a few months ago. The twins' other siblings are much younger and not as close to the twins as Fendi is. I don't know how I feel about Fendi coming over to spend the night, but I'll do anything for my kids. Our family is certainly a blended bunch.

"Mommy and Mr. Frederick said it's fine if it's okay with you," Ace throws in. He's sitting on the couch in my office playing on his iPad. A'Mya is right next to him doing the same.

I groan internally. Having a third kid in the house is sure to up the chaos. I already know they're going to stay up all night playing Roblox and sneaking snacks. Something I would do at their age.

I pick up my cellphone on my desk to send Sasha a text confirming Fendi spending the night. I have a few emails I want to respond to before we leave in less than an hour.

There's a knock on my office door. "Come in!" I call out.

Tanya walks in looking good as always in a sleeveless pink dress and heels. I stand up to greet her with a smile instantly gracing my face. I'm always happy to see her.

"Hey baby," I reply, forgetting the twins are in my office.

Tanya halts her steps when she notices them though. Ace and A'Mya's heads are lifted from their devices, looking at her expectantly. They have never seen me smitten with a woman. Ever.

I hadn't thought much about when I would introduce Tanya to the twins, so now is as good as ever. My feelings run deep for this woman, and I want my children to know it.

"Ace, A'Mya, this is Miss Tanya, my girlfriend." I round my desk to walk over to Tanya. She looks from me to the twins.

"Girlfriend? You got a girlfriend, Daddy? She's pretty!" A'Mya bounces up from the couch, then launches against Tanya, startling her with a hug around her waist.

"Oh my," Tanya giggles off the nerves I bet she was feeling seconds ago. "You are pretty too, A'Mya. It's nice to meet you."

"You pulled a baddie, Dad!" Ace shocks the heck out of me.

A'Mya giggles.

I ask, "Boy, what you know about a baddie?" Tanya and I laugh as Ace gets his turn giving her a hug.

"It's nice to meet you, Ace. You're handsome like your dad."

Ace strokes his chin. "Thanks."

Yo, what affect does my woman have on my son?

I gently pull Tanya into a hug before kissing her briefly on the lips. Keeping it PG.

"I'm sorry, I didn't know your kids were here," Tanya says softly against my ear.

"No worries. Now was the perfect time for you to meet them. They're in love with you already." I snip her ear before stepping out of our embrace.

"Yeah…I ran into Corine on my way over here with her trifling behind. I'll tell you about it later."

"Do you and my daddy go on dates, Miss Tanya?" A'Mya takes Tanya's hand, tugging her over to the couch to sit next to her.

"Yes, we do."

"Is he romantic?" My daughter continues with the questions.

Tanya blushes. "Very romantic. He's always a gentleman.

"He buys you flowers and opens your doors?" Ace asks, obviously interested in the conversation too.

"Yes, he does."

"Good. That's how he tells me to treat a girl," Ace says.

"Your dad is teaching you well, Ace. It's always good to be a gentleman."

"Will it get me a girlfriend pretty and nice like you one day?" Ace asks, hopeful.

Tanya looks over at me before answering him. I give her a wink. "Yes, Ace. I bet you won't have any problems finding a good girlfriend when the time is right."

I go back to sit behind my desk to finish replying to emails as Tanya and my children get to know each other.

Thank you, Lord!

10
ANTWAIN

"I hope Miss Tanya loves her surprise, Dad," Ace says when I park the Expedition in front of Sasha's mansion.

"She's gonna love it. I'm a girl, so I know." A'Mya unbuckles her seatbelt.

I love the bond they have developed with Tanya these past few months. Today is me and Tanya's six months anniversary and I have a special evening planned. Which is why I'm dropping them off at their mother's house.

We get out the SUV and I help them carry their things. Sasha answers the door after the third ring. Her five-year-old son is clinging to her pants. He excitedly hugs his older siblings when they walk in.

"Yay! Ace and Mya here!" He tugs both their arms, dragging them away.

"Bye, Dad!" the twins yell in unison.

"Why are you dropping them off two hours early?" Sasha asks with an attitude, looking me up and down.

"I thought it was cool. I got something to do."

"Or someone," she says under her breath, but I hear her clearly. I ignore it because I legit have no interest in what's going on inside her head unless it pertains to my children.

Sasha has been coming at me with a funky attitude for weeks now. I don't know what her problem is. Despite how our marriage ended, over the years, we have managed to co-parent without major issues. So this is new.

"Do I need to get them and wait two hours until it's your turn to be a parent?" I regret my words before I finish saying them. She unfortunately has been pushing my buttons for a while and I allow my pettiness to kick in.

"Really, Antwain? They're here now, aren't they?" Sasha sucks her teeth.

"Yet, you're acting like it's an inconvenience. I'll see you on Sunday." I turn to leave.

"Whatever!" She slams the door as soon as I step onto the porch.

I shake my head. *Maybe she needs Freddy to give her some viagra dick...okay Lord, forgive my pettiness.*

I hop in my ride to head back home. Tanya is coming over tonight. We've been great about not spending excessive time alone in each other's homes because temptation is real whenever I'm in her presence. I wanna devour her – nice and slow. We haven't crossed the line—thank God for His mercy. We won't compromise ourselves tonight either. I have a private chef preparing our meals in my kitchen now. He should be done by the time I get back.

If I didn't think Tanya would turn me down because it's too soon, I would pop the question to her tonight. I'll wait a little longer. I want to ensure it's not my boy down south taking the lead in wanting to make her my wife.

About an hour later, I'm freshly showered and dressed nicely in slacks and a polo shirt. Tanya loves when I have my tattooed arm sleeve on display. My entire left arm is covered in tats. I've been toying with the idea of adding a tattoo that represents Tanya somewhere on my left shoulder.

The doorbell sounds just as my feet hit the last step coming down from upstairs in my bedroom. I know it's my baby. She caught an Uber here so I can take her home later tonight.

"God, you are good..." I bite down on my lip, admiring the feminine masterpiece standing on my porch.

We're gonna stay celibate. We're gonna stay celibate, I remind myself.

Tanya has me ready to risk it all. She's looking too good in this purple romper, jumpsuit or whatever you call the one-piece pants thingy she's rocking.

"You like?" Tanya steps into the house and I check her out further from behind.

I now know why David got caught slipping with Bathsheba. *Lord, the way you built women makes them kryptonite.*

"Baby, you are gorgeous." I secure the door then take her into my arms for a hug then a quick kiss. "Happy six months anniversary. I love you!" I had planned to reveal my true feelings at dinner, but it slipped.

"Antwain, babe," Tanya looks up at me. "I love you too! So much." Her eyes fill with happy tears.

I swipe the droplets away before indulging in a deep kiss, backing her against the door. I gently grip her neck, squeezing, then angle her head just where I want it to properly feast on her lips and sweet tongue. All her lipstick vanishes.

With us both knowing our limits, we separate our lips, breathing deeply.

"So, dinner smells good," Tanya tries to divert our desire for each other. It's another tactic we use to remain faithful to our vow of celibacy.

"Yeah. I got lobster for you, baby."

"Yeeee!" Tanya squeals, clapping her hands animatedly. She loves seafood.

I take her hand, leading her to the dining room. It's decorated with different shades of aster flowers. The lady at the floral shop told me they are September flowers and symbolize a strong and powerful love. It's the same type of love I have for Tanya.

"Wow, Antwain. These flowers are beautiful!" Tanya gushes, walking over to the large floral arrangement in the center of the dining table. She touches the flower petals before leaning in to smell the fragrance.

I pull the ring box out my pocket. Nothing is going as I planned it. I'm too eager to wait until after dinner to express my true desires for this woman. I step closer to her to place a kiss on her bare shoulder.

"Is – is that what I think it is?" Tanya asks after turning around to see the jewelry box in my hand.

"Not quite. It's a promise ring." I flip the box open, revealing the diamond eternity ring.

Tanya's mouth drops open in awe. "It's beautiful, babe."

I take the ring from the box, then I reach for her hand. "Tanya, this ring symbolizes my love for you and my promise to make you Mrs. Hall in the very near future, if you'll have me." I look into her eyes, eagerly anticipating her answer.

"Yes! I would marry you today, baby. But I know we should wait a bit longer. We can go to the courthouse soon to get our marriage certificate, just to have it ready."

I happily slip the ring on her finger. I pick her up to seal the promise with a kiss.

11
TANYA

"Oh my, Tanya, that's the one!" Janet gushes.

"I agree. It fits you perfectly!" My mom wipes tears from her eyes. She's sixty-nine and fine with her head full of gray hair that women half her age are trying to rival with hair dyes and weaves.

I stare at myself in the full-length mirror. This A-line strapless gown looks like it's made specifically for me.

I wonder what Antwain would think.

"I don't know many women who buy a wedding dress before getting engaged. If you were with any other man, I would put you in a headlock to talk some sense into you. But Antwain is A-1. And I'm not saying that just because he's a pastor. 'Cause unfortunately, some of them I would run from."

"Preach!" Mommy cosigns. "My sweet Tanya. Your daddy would be so happy to see you in your wedding dress. You rededicated your life to Christ and soon you will be marrying a godly man. I'm happy for you."

"Mommy, you're going to make me cry." I fan my face to help ward off my tears. It's not working.

We took the train from DC to New York for the weekend to find me a dress. This is the seventh one I have tried on. There's no need to look any further.

I'm in an amazing place in my life right now – emotionally, spiritually, financially and romantically. I couldn't be happier…well, I can when Antwain and I celebrate our love in marriage.

"Are you saying yes to the dress?" the helpful bridal consultant asks.

I look at her through the reflection in the mirror. "Yes. I'm saying yes to the dress."

She beams. "Wonderful. We will make the alternations then ship the dress out to you. After you change, we can arrange payment."

This dress is almost ten thousand dollars and worth every penny my frugal behind will pay.

"What are your pet peeves in a relationship, Tanya?" Dr. Scott asks. She is a black and Asian woman in her early fifties and came highly recommended.

This is me and Antwain's fourth session with her for pre-martial counselling. Today is the last Monday in November. We're not engaged yet, but after Antwain gave me my promise ring two months ago, I insisted we start sessions. When he pops the question, I want us both to be properly prepared to take that big step. I'm not having a long engagement. I'm almost forty-six years old I want to start my happily ever after right away.

I play with my fingers in my lap as I think about the question. Antwain is sitting beside me, with Dr. Scott sitting in her swivel desk chair across from us. "Clothes being left on the floor after changing." I cringe. "It's a biggie for me."

Antwain looks guilty as he playfully tries to cover his face in shame. "I'm not that bad, but I would admit I have my moments. To my defense, I just be too tired sometimes, but I do take care of it the next day.”

“Well, you’re definitely not a pig from what I’ve seen being at your house. As long as you don’t leave your clothes on the floor for long, I can handle it.”

Dr. Scott directs the same question to Antwain. “What about you, Antwain. Any pet peeves in a relationship?”

“Moving my things without putting them back in their place. That would drive me crazy,” Antwain admits.

“What if I’m borrowing a razor?” I ask.

“In that case, you can keep the razor. But anything else, please return it.”

“Got it!”

“Okay, now both of you, what are your expectations on sex? Though sex isn’t the most important aspect in marriage, it’s high on the list, and having realistic and common expectations helps.”

Antwain clears his throat. "I expect to have a healthy and active sex life. I would want it regularly during the week. At least five times. I'm open to exploring ways to be intimate with each other without any third parties involved. I know there are peaks and valleys in a relationship, and it would affect our sex life, but I always want us to be open and honest with each other about our desires."

"I'm one hundred percent in agreement with that. I'm not into the whips and chains and adding anybody else, but I'm open minded about exploring ways to fulfill each other's desires."

"Now, are there any health concerns either of you need to reveal to each other?" Dr. Scott asks, crossing one leg over the other.

"Nothing other than the fact that I'm at that age of perimenopause. I haven't experienced any negative symptoms from it though. I hope it stays that way."

My only major change is irregular periods. I hope I never have to deal with hot flashes and mood swings. My mom didn't, which makes me hopeful that I won't either.

"Even if you do experience any symptoms, know that I will take care of you. Just don't freeze my butt off during hot flashes," Antwain grins.

I playfully slap his arm. "Shut up!" I laugh.

"I don't have any known health issues. And you know I stay fit by going to the gym a few times a week," Antwain says to me.

"Good, good. Our time for the day is almost done. Do either of you have anything you would like to discuss before we end?" Dr. Scott asks.

Antwain shakes his head.

"I do…I'm concerned about what co-parenting with Antwain's ex-wife would be like. When Antwain and I get married, I will be spending more time with the twins— more than their mom, in fact, since Antwain has full custody. I don't want any drama."

Antwain reaches for my hand in my lap. He laces our fingers together. "For the most part, Sasha and I have done great with co-parenting. Though recently, she's been acting weird and getting upset over petty things. Regardless, Sasha will respect your position in my life. The twins love you and talk about you all the time. I'm sure they've told Sasha about you already. I can plan a dinner with her and her husband for me to introduce you."

I nod, liking what he's saying. If we're planning a future together, I must meet the mother of his children.

I just hope Sasha's not with the BS.

12
ANTWAIN

From the kitchen, I hear the front door open, followed by footsteps. It's the twins. I left the door unlocked because I knew Sasha was on her way bringing them home. I close the fridge after getting a bottled water, then head toward the front.

"Hey, Daddy," the twins say in unison, giving me a hug.

"What's up? You all enjoy your weekend?"

"Yeah."

"It was cool."

They head toward the stairs to go to their rooms, lugging their weekend bags.

I look back at Sasha. "Hey, can you wait a sec? I want to talk to you about something."

"Yeah, sure," Sasha is standing near the front door.

"A'Mya and Ace, put your things away, then pack your bags for school tomorrow," I call out.

"Okay, Dad."

"All right."

I gesture for Sasha to step out onto the front porch. I do the same, closing the door behind us.

"What's up?" She leans against the porch railing.

"I want to have dinner with you and Frederick to introduce you to my woman," I say, matter of factually.

Sasha looks taken aback and seems to instantly get defensive. "Your woman? Is she the one the twins have been talking about? Tina or something?"

I have a feeling she knows Tanya's name, but I'll let that slide.

"Her name is Tanya. We've been dating for eight months. It's serious, so I want you to meet the woman that I'm in love with and who's around our kids."

"In love?" She scrunches her nose in disgust. "It's been eight years and you're just now seeing someone new and you're in love?"

"I bet you liked it that way, didn't you? You moved on with someone new and I didn't. Rest assured, it wasn't because I couldn't find someone better."

Sasha eyes thin evilly as she looks at me. "Whatever, Antwain. I'll meet your li'l girlfriend. Text me when and where and I'll let you know if my husband and I are available."

I smirk. "Yeah, you do that. Peace." I chuck the deuces then head back inside.

I want to finish up a sermon I was working on before I spend a few hours with the twins before bed.

✳✳✳

If Sasha wasn't feeling some type of way already about the new woman in my life, she may blow a gasket when she sees how extra fine Tanya is looking tonight in the African print pantsuit she's wearing for dinner. She makes me look good.

"You trying to make an everlasting impression tonight I see," I joke again with Tanya as we walk hand in hand into the swanky restaurant. She and I really don't care where we eat as long as the food is good.

Sasha and her husband are a bit too bourgie, which is why I chose this place in DC for dinner. You can't enter the establishment unless you're dressed to impress.

"Oh, this old thing? Just something I picked up in Johannesburg a while back."

I chuckle as we're escorted to our table. Frederick and Sasha are already seated. The moment Sasha spots us, her mouth pinches together as if she's sucking on sour candy. I shouldn't get this much pleasure from seeing my ex-wife squirm, but I do. I really do think she's enjoyed the fact that I've been single all these years while she's had a happy life with Frederick.

Frederick stands when we get to the table. Sasha remains seated, sizing Tanya up.

"Hey, Frederick," I greet him.

"Hey." We shake hands then he extends a hand to Tanya. "I'm Sasha's husband. It's nice to meet you."

Tanya accepts his handshake. "I'm Tanya. It's nice to meet you too."

Frederick turns to his bitter wife. "Sasha, don't be rude."

Sasha stands begrudgingly, plastering a fake smile on her face. "Hello, Tasha. Nice outfit. You got it from Wal-Mart?"

If she only knew Tanya's net worth is most likely greater than her and her husband's. Despite pursing a nursing degree during our marriage, Sasha gave up on college after marrying Frederick and becoming first lady of his church.

"Don't be hating on Wal-Mart. But no, I got this during one of my trips to Johannesburg. Have you visited before?" Tanya replies with class.

"I'm too busy being a *wife*, *mother* and *first lady* of a mega church to be globetrotting," Sasha replies snidely.

I catch Sasha's eyes, giving her a warning.

Frederick clears his throat. "Have a seat. The waiter should be back soon to take our orders."

They return to their seats while I pull out Tanya's chair before sitting beside her at the square table across from Frederick and Sasha.

There's a brief awkward silence as we browse the menu before the waiter comes to take our orders. Frederick helps break the ice with engaging small talk until our food arrives.

"What is the purpose of this dinner?" Sasha asks after we've said grace and begun eating.

"Tanya is an important part of my life and future, and I wanted us all to meet since we play important roles in the twins' lives." I cut into my steak.

"I've heard them mention you a few times, Tanya. They seem to really love you." Frederick picks up his glass of whatever he ordered for a sip.

"I love them too." Tanya beams. "I don't have children, but if I did, I would've wanted a perfect pair like them."

"Since you don't have any children, just be clear on the fact that I'm their mother, not you! Don't come around them acting like you're the main woman in their lives." Sasha shouts from across the table, garnering stares from people at the other tables around us.

Where the heck did that come from?

"Relax, sweetheart." Frederick turns Sasha's head to look at him. "Her role in their lives will be the same as mine. No one can take your place as their mother."

I place my hand on Tanya's leg that's bouncing profusely. I know she's fighting with all the angels to stop some profanities from spewing from her mouth. Because a few choice words popped in my head too.

"Yo, you need to chill, Sasha. I didn't come at your husband sideways when he became stepdaddy. Matter of fact, I didn't get the same curtesy of a proper introduction like I'm giving you. Yes, you are the twin's mother, and no one is trying to threaten that. But you will respect the fact that Tanya will be a big part of their lives as a stepparent. She won't be doing anything I wouldn't want Frederick to do."

Sasha rolls her eyes. "I don't even know why I'm all worked up. Y'all not even engaged. She'll be history soon as you get bored with her." She flicks her wrist in a dismissive way.

"Bitc –" Tanya pushes away from the table. "You know what? I'm not going to stoop to your pathetic level because this isn't about me. It's about something your husband needs to be concerned about. But sorry boo, Antwain is *my* man. You threw away a good man, now you're in your feelings now that he's found me. A woman who knows his worth and won't give him up." Tanya stands. "It was nice meeting you, Pastor Frederick. Good night." She snatches her purse off the table. "I'll meet you up front, Antwain."

I mentally fist pump the air. *That's my woman right there!*

"Nah, I'm coming with you." I stand then pull out my wallet to grab a few hundreds to throw on the table. "Tanya will be my wife, so get used to that fact." I take Tanya's hand then we walk away from the table.

"Is there something you need to tell me?" I hear Frederick ask Sasha as we leave.

Like it or not, Sasha, Tanya is here to stay.

13
ANTWAIN

I arrive at the dealership a little after twelve today. I spent the morning in meetings with three individuals from the congregation. Two gentlemen and a lady. Alicia, of course, remained in the church office during that time with my office door wide open. Alicia can't hear, but she can see what's happening during my meetings with women. I don't play those games of getting caught up in compromising situations with my reputation on the line.

"Good afternoon, Mr. Antwain," my assistant, Kirk, says when I walk into the reception area of the executive office. The interior decorator came and decorated my office for Christmas, as well as the entire dealership. Mariah Carey's, "All I Want for Christmas is You" is playing on the surround sound speakers. I love the festivities of this time of year. Though I believe the birth of Christ shouldn't only be celebrated in December.

"Good day, Mr. Kirk," I greet him. We have a relaxed work environment, but I insist that everyone addresses each other respectfully. It seems to work, because between that and the high wages, there's no major turnovers on employment here.

"I left your messages on your desk, Sir." He's sitting behind his own desk.

"'Preciate it." I step into my office, walking slowly to my desk while appreciating the manifestation of what I'd prayed for. This was only by the grace of God and ain't nothing cliché about that.

When Sasha packed up her things and left, it made me go deeper into my faith and grind harder for the things I knew God laid on my heart to accomplish with my life. Things were rough for a long time though. I was a broke, divorced, single dad, but I couldn't give up on my dreams. For myself, and Ace and A'Mya. The hard work paid off – tremendously.

Less than an hour later, Kirk is calling me on my desk phone. "Yes," I answer while looking at my computer screen at some sales reports.

"There's a Ms. Sasha here to see you, Sir."

What is she doing here?

"Send her in, thanks." I hang up the phone, turning my attention to my closed office door. Seconds later, I watch the door handle shift as someone pushes it open.

"Wow." Sasha looks around my office in amazement while stepping in, then closes the door behind her. "I can't believe this is my first time coming to your dealership. Your office is tastefully decorated. You must refer the interior decorator to me."

I roll my eyes away from her pretentiousness to close out the screen on my computer. Sasha only became bourgie after marrying money.

"What do you want, Sasha?" I ask flippantly. Something tells me this has nothing to do with our kids. I lean comfortably against my chair, eager for her to get to the point then leave.

"Really, Antwain? Can't you and I socialize outside of our children?" She takes a seat in one of the armchairs in front of my desk. Her expense perfume assaults my nostrils as she does so.

"No. Our co-parenting works just fine as it is. Are you here to apologize for your behavior at dinner a week ago?"

"Hell no! For what?" She lifts her bare leg to cross over the other. It's hard not to notice the mini skirt and matching jacket she's wearing. It's the second week of December. It's cold! Yet, here she is dressed like its summer.

"Disrespecting my future wife, that's what! The only person who can threaten your position in our children's lives is you. Respect what I have going on with Tanya the same way I respect your marriage."

"Are you serious about her, Antwain? I mean, coming as the woman who once carried your last name and the mother of your two children, don't you think you're rushing things with her? You've been dating for less than a year and already you're referring to her as your future wife?" Sasha has an "are you stupid" look on her face.

I regard her for a moment. "How long did it take you to get married to Frederick, Sasha? A day, or was it five?"

She visibly swallows, a telltale of me pulling her card. As if I can forget that not even a full week after our divorce was final, she married her husband.

"That's dif–"

"That's bull and her stank sister shit and I don't associate with either one of them, Sasha," I grit through my teeth. Yes, I have forgiven her, but I haven't forgotten. Which is why I can't ever see us being friends as she suggested.

Lord, help tame my attitude. How dare she act as if she's concerned about my best interest when she's the one who hurt me the most.

"I'm sorry I hurt you all those years ago, Antwain. I was young, immature and selfish. I can admit that. I have regretted what I did to you for a long time…"

Yet you've never apologized until today and I'm not even sure it's sincere.

"...I shouldn't have given up on us...on you...on our family. But I was scared that we would never accomplish all the plans we made for our future. I met Frederick by chance one day while at the grocery store. He saw me struggling with the twins and trying to load the groceries in the trunk. He helped me...then we just started talking. I didn't tell him I was married..."

"Sasha, I don't want to hear this. What's done is done."

"I know. All I'm trying to do is say that I'm truly sorry for hurting you and throwing our marriage away...I made a mistake and I want us to be a family again."

Say what now?

My face scrunches in a frown at her audacity. "Do I need to make recommendations for a psychiatrist?" I'm dead serious 'cause she must have lost her mind.

Sasha uncrosses her legs to lean forward in the seat. "I'm serious, Antwain. I want us to be a family again. I don't think I ever stopped loving you."

I chuckle as a way to stop myself from cussing her out in proper fluency. Moments like these, I wish it was easy for me to put my faith aside to be the devil's puppet just for a minute or two to get this pressure building up off my chest.

"Refrain from anger, and forsake wrath! Fret not yourself; it tends only to evil." Psalm 37:8. I allow the Scripture to roll in my thoughts a few times to calm the beast roaring inside me.

"Sasha, let's pretend for a moment that I would slightly entertain what you're saying. Why would you think I would want to be with a woman who can so easily walk away from her marriage and children? Should I take turn now being stepfather to your other three children? Frederick and I will switch roles and we'll be a happy, dysfunctional family?"

More and more I've realized how she did me a favor by packing her things and divorcing me all those years ago. God knew she wasn't right for me. Apparently not Frederick either. But she's his problem now.

"We can make it work." She smiles like she's got it all figured out. She leans back, spreading her legs apart as her skirt rides up further on her thighs. Her yellow panties are hard to miss, and I'm not even trying to see them.

I have zero interest in this bootleg movie scene from *Basic Instinct* that she's enacting. "Get your shi – leave my office Sasha, now!" I bark. I stand up. "Don't you ever disrespect me like this again. The only thing I want from you is to be a good mother to our children and for us to co-parent cordially. I'm dead on anything else."

"You know you still love me, Antwain. Just admit it, then we can figure out how to be a family again."

I'mma need Frederick to get his wife committed.

I round my desk to run up on her, gently snatching her up from the seat. "I don't love you, Sasha. Definitely not in the way you think. I don't want you and I haven't wanted you since you left me. You're jealous of Tanya. I can understand that. But don't project that into something more. There will never be a 'you and me' ever again. You made sure of that. Go home to your husband and other three children. Ask your husband for forgiveness and y'all work on your marriage."

Tears well in Sasha's eyes. "Oh God," she sobs. "I'm…I can't believe I made a fool of myself." She covers her face with her hands when I step out of her personal space. "I've…I haven't seen you with anyone else since me and I just…I don't know. I'm sorry. I don't know what I was thinking coming here. I love Frederick, I really do. But things between us have been different the older he gets –"

"A'ight. I'm not the one to pour your heart out to. Go to confessional with your husband." I snatch my office door open for her to leave.

Sasha frantically wipes the tears from her eyes before picking up her purse off the chair. She walks over to me at the door. "Antwain, please forgive me. I'm serious. I'm really sorry for my behavior at dinner and today…Tell Tanya I'm sorry too."

"I'll appreciate it if you tell her that yourself. I forgive you. Don't relapse again."

She faintly smiles at my crack at her. "I won't. You're a good man and father. Tanya is blessed to have you." Sasha leaves and I waste no time shutting the door behind her.

I pray the rest of my day is a breeze after that.

14
TANYA

"I'm going to tell Pastor Tim that you're cheating on him. This is your fourth Sunday coming to church with me."

Mom and I exit my car, making sure our winter coats are properly shielding us from this early February cold. I automatically hit the locks on my key fob while we walk toward the church entrance.

"Pastor Tim knows I'm a loyal member. I'm not going nowhere. But the series Antwain has been preaching on these past weeks has me hooked."

It has me hooked too. Antwain has been preaching from the book of Songs of Solomon. The book of love. I'm not gonna lie, his teaching from this book of the Bible feels so intimate when he addresses the congregation. It feels as if he's speaking specifically to me.

We can hear Minister Fiona closing the announcements and welcoming the choir to the stage.

I don't have time to make my weekly pit stop to Antwain's office before church service, but I have a dedicated seat in the row behind him. Because we're not engaged or married, I choose not to sit beside him during service. Our relationship is no secret. The congregation knows their single pastor has a woman in his life.

Mom and I greet others as we enter the sanctuary. Church is full as usual. Because there's only one Sunday service, people do well showing up on time 'cause they know that's how the church service is run – on time. Antwain and the church board don't play with that fashionably late nonsense. Respect is given to people's time. I absolutely love it.

The choir sets the mood for praise and worship. I lift my arms, sing and rejoice.

Lord, You are worthy of all praise and honor. Thank You for Your loving kindness. Thank You for not giving up on me, and welcoming me back into Your loving arms. I no longer want to do things my way, Lord. I want to honor You with my time, talent, and life. Have Your way in my life…

"The final topic on this series from the book of Songs of Solomon is, 'True Love is Worth Waiting for'…" Antwain addresses the congregation looking fly as ever in his three-piece suit. "Let's read together from Songs of Solomon two verse seven…"

"Daughters of Jerusalem, I charge you by the gazelles and by the does of the field: Do not arouse or awaken love until it so desires."

"Several times in this book of the Bible, the Shulamite wife urges young, single women to wait for love…romance…sex. She pleads with them to take their time in pursuit of true love. Why? She wanted to warn them of the destruction it would cause if they gave in to their desires instead of waiting for the right time…waiting on God's timing."

Antwain looks about the congregation before his eyes settle on me. "We must wait for God's good and perfect will for our lives. Wait for the one He has destined us to find. You see, God gave us these desires for a reason. He wants us to find love and happiness with another, yet He also wants to help us avoid heartache in the pursuit of it. Waiting is not easy. I'm a testament to that. But it's so worth it…" Antwain smiles before looking away from me.

Mom nudges me with her elbow. "Don't be thinking naughty stuff in the house of the Lord," she whispers.

Busted!

I tune back into what Antwain is saying to stop my dirty train of thought. Hearing him preach always arouses me. *He needs to propose already.*

The service eventually comes to an end. I expect people to be standing to leave, yet it seems I'm the only one gathering my things. I look over at mom and she's sitting there like it's not time to go.

"Is there going to be a presentation I don't know ab–" My question to my mom is cut off by the choir singing, "I Found Love" by BeBe Winans. My heart starts beating quickly. This is the exact song I sent to Antwain a few weeks ago expressing my love for him.

Mom reaches for my hand as I collapse back into my seat. She gives it a gentle squeeze while smiling at me. Others around us are looking at me as if they're all in on something.

This is it. Oh my goodness, this is it!

Antwain seems to materialize out of nowhere, standing beside me. Tears of joy pool in my eyes.

"Tanya Anastacia Freeman…" He kneels.

I think I'm about to pass out from excitement and anticipation.

Antwain takes my free hand as my mother releases my other one. "There's no doubt in my heart and mind that you are the one God had me wait for. You're the one He wants me to love and cherish. To support you and honor you all the days of my life. I'm in love with you, baby. The twins love you too –"

"We do!" Ace and A'Mya shout, causing the congregation to applaud. I'm just now noticing them standing next to Mr. and Mrs. Hall and Alicia with her husband and children.

My eyes widen when I see Janet and her man not far from Antwain's family. Everyone was really in on this.

Antwain continues. "…We want you to be a part of our family. Will you do us the honor of being my wife?" He reaches into his pocket pulling out the most perfect engagement ring for me. It's simple and exquisite.

"Yes!! You should've been asked me!" I exclaim throwing my arms around his neck, bypassing him putting the ring on my finger. The congregation shouts with applause.

Antwain chuckles, then kisses the side of my neck. "Thank you, baby. Now let me finalize our commitment by putting the ring on your finger."

I lean out of our embrace to allow him the honor of slipping the ring on my bare left finger. The promise ring is on my right.

"Okay, now when's the wedding?" Janet shouts over the celebratory greetings Antwain and I are receiving.

"I think today is a good day for one, if you ask me. But that's up to the engaged couple," Mrs. Hall replies.

What are they doing?

With us both now standing, Antwain smiles at me with a mischievous look on his face. "I'm with mom. Today is a pretty good day to make you my wife."

"I don't have my dress and we would need a photographer –"

"It's all covered sweetheart, so is that a yes or a no?" Mom asks.

Everyone seems to be anticipating my answer.

"Yes!"

Another roar of celebration.

"Let's get them married," Mr. Hall yells. "Decorators you've got thirty minutes to transform the sanctuary. Ladies take the bride-to-be to get dolled up. Son, do we need to have a talk about the birds and the bees since it's been a while?"

Antwain's best friend, Ezra, howls with laughter which causes a domino effect.

15
ANTWAIN

Now why did Tanya have to do me like this?

My mouth drops when she appears in the doorway of the sanctuary. She's extraordinarily stunning in her wedding gown. Like how is it possible for her to look better every time I see her?

God, thank You for this amazing gift. My bride.

I get choked up with tears while Tanya walks forward to the instrumental music with her mother by her side. Ezra pats my back in support. The photographer doesn't miss a beat capturing the moment.

I've done this wedding thing once before – now feels so much different. It feels right. Maybe it's my maturity. Maybe it's my stronger faith. Maybe it's the *woman*.

Tanya mouths, *I love you*, when she's a couple steps away. She too has tears in her eyes.

I place a kiss on Mrs. Freeman's cheek after she hands Tanya over to me. "Thank you. I promise I will do right by your daughter."

"I trust you will, *son*." Mrs. Freeman gives me a confident smile before stepping back.

I look over at Tanya. I get emotional all over again now that she's beside me, at the altar. "You're beautiful."

"Thank you. Your tears say it all. And you, of course, are dressed handsomely for the occasion. Now I know why you wore this three-piece suit today."

"Are you sure this wedding isn't too soon?" This was all sprung on her less than an hour ago and if she wants more time to plan our wedding, I'll wait, even though I don't want to.

Tanya shakes her head. "No. The timing is perfect."

"Ahh, hmm." My dad clears his throat to get our attention. He will be marrying us today. He too is an ordained minister. I couldn't think of any other person to do the honor. "This is going to be short and sweet. You two can resume your conversation shortly."

The audience laughs.

Twenty minutes later…

"I now pronounce you, Mr. and Mrs. Antwain and Tanya Hall!"

I pick Tanya up bridal style. She giggles because of my jovial expression of love. Our guests cheer loudly. I plant my lips against hers, kissing her deeply. She returns the gesture, palming the back of head to pull me closer, or to hold me tighter – either way I'm enjoying it.

✷✷✷

"Do we call you mom?" Ace asks Tanya as my family of four dances together at our reception.

We're the only ones on the dancefloor moving to the beat of "We are Family" by Sister Sledge. Tanya and Ace are dancing together and A'Mya and I are dancing with each other.

"No. I'm your stepmom. Your mom, Sasha, holds the title of mom. Maybe we can come up with a different name for me," Tanya says.

"What about…mum? Like British people say mom," A'Mya suggests.

I like the idea. Oddly, the twins never mentioned wanting to call Frederick "Papa" or anything like that. Honestly, with the way Sasha left me for him, I would've lost it if they wanted to call him anything but Mr. Frederick. Maybe in some ways, Sasha knew that wouldn't go over well, which is why it was never an issue. I wouldn't trip now if they wanted to. Despite the spanking episode, Frederick has been a solid dude when it comes to the twins.

"Yeah, what about mum?" Ace asks, looking hopeful.

Tanya smiles. "Sure. You can call me mum."

"I'm so happy you're our mum!" A'Mya steps away from me to give my wife a bear hug.

"Me too," Ace hugs the other side of Tanya.

"I am too. I love you both so much. I look forward to being your bonus mom."

✳✳✳

It feels as if my dick is about to break off because it's so hard. I have never anticipated making love this badly in all my sexual experienced life. I want…need my wife.

I step out the hotel suite bathroom, no longer able to wait for Tanya's surprise. She's bent over trying to get her shapely leg into piece of white material. I couldn't care less about lingerie right now. With bare feet against the plush carpet, I sneak up on her, scooping her up as she yelps.

"Antwain! No, I'm still getting ready."

I gently place her on the king-sized bed with fancy expensive covers. "You're ready baby, trust. I can't wait any longer. I promise you can put on all that fancy stuff you brought later. I'm ready to feast now." I practically growl, looking down at her glorious naked body that the good Lord created for me.

Tanya lustfully scans my bare body. Her teeth sink deeply into her bottom lip when she sees my saluted friend. Her soft hands caress it, causing me to hiss in pleasure. I let her have her fun.

"My turn." I nudge her to lay on her back. She obliges, spreading wide.

"God bless," she says before I proceed to eat. I love a woman with good manners, but we about to get nasty.

16
TANYA

It's been two months since our "I do's." I've moved in with Antwain and the twins. My house is now rental income for us through Airbnb. It took me a few weeks to get used to a full house after living the single and children-free life for so many years. We now have a good rhythm to our new family.

I take turns with Antwain taking the twins to and from school and extracurricular activities, which I enjoy. I love cooking meals with my family and eating dinner together. I've wanted to be a mom for so long, so being mum to the twins is a new joy in my life.

If we wait on the Lord to manifest the things He has for us, they will all happen in due season. I'm finally in the season I prayed for in my youth. I want to enjoy every moment of it.

Though I'm married to a pastor, I haven't taken on the "traditional" or "expected" role of first lady. I still volunteer for Sunday school, but I'm not on any church boards, nor have I taken on the women's ministry responsibility. I enjoy helping in the church, but God didn't call me to ministry—he called my husband. Some of the people my husband deals with in the church make me want to cuss them out. I don't know how he does it.

Antwain and I have been humping like rabbits since our wedding night. We try to keep things tame when the kids are around, but when they're with their mother and Frederick – oh it's on and popping. Tonight is going to be one of those nights.

"Hi, husband," I answer Antwain's call. I call him husband every chance I get. I'm in our home office doing some consultant work for HireRight.

"Hey, cougar." He hasn't dropped his pet name for me. I love it. "Can you pick the twins up from school then take them to their mom for five? I've got a mini crisis going on here at church."

"Sure, I can get the twins. But what's going on?"

Antwain sighs deeply. I imagine him pinching the bridge of his nose. "Pastor Tommy just punched Brother George in the mouth 'cause he thinks Brother George is trying to push up on his wife. So we had to break up two fifty-year-old men from fighting. Then Sister Paula blurts out she's pregnant because she'd been keeping it a secret for weeks. Now she's afraid of being asked to step down from the church board. On top of that, she said she doesn't know who the father is…"

Yikes!

This is why we need the church; we aren't perfect, and we need Jesus.

"Yeah, you've got a situation going on right there. God's going to give you wisdom on how to handle it."

"I'm going to need all His wisdom and grace for sure. Thanks for getting the twins."

"No problem, husband. I love you."

"I love you too. I hope to be home no later than seven. You gon' be ready for me?" His voice drops a few octaves, sending a thrill up my spine.

"You know I will.

"Wear that thing I like."

"Of course. I will be butterball naked."

I pull up to Sasha and Frederick's home at 4:56 pm. Me and Sasha haven't had much of an interaction since the first time we met at dinner. Antwain told me all about her visit to his office at the dealership, making a fool of herself. Apparently, she and Frederick worked out their marital issues, or they're ignoring them because they're still together and appear to be doing fine.

Sasha pitched a fit when she found out Ace and A'Mya call me mum. It took the twins explaining why for her to chill. Honestly, if she had wanted them to stop, I would've been fine. I truly don't want to overstep my bounds and offend her as their mother.

My relationship with the twins is solid enough that I don't need the title of mum.

"Make sure you grab all of your things," I tell the twins before we exit the car.

"I have my things," Ace says.

"Me too," A'Mya says.

We head up the steps to the front door. Ace rings the doorbell. We can hear someone approaching the door before it's swung open. Sasha's in the doorway with a faint smile on her face when she notices me.

I wave. She gives me a head nod.

"Hi, my babies." She opens her arms to welcome the twins in for a hug. She kisses both of their foreheads.

"Hi, mom," they reply in unison.

"Your brothers and sister are in the playroom," she tells them.

"Okay." Ace turns to me. "Bye, mum." We fist bump. It's our thing.

"See you on Sunday…You too A'Mya."

"Bye, mum." A'Mya and I link our pinkies together. It's our thing.

The twins turn then walk away to find their siblings. I turn to leave too.

"Hey, just a sec." Sasha stops me from retreating. I turn back to face her. She steps on the porch, closing the door behind her. "I never did congratulate you and Antwain on your marriage. Congratulations. You've married a good man."

"Thank you. I know."

She sighs. "Look, in the beginning I can admit I was jealous when really, I had no right to be. I left Antwain and moved on with my life. I'm sorry for my behavior towards you. Like you said, it wasn't about you, it was about me. Now that you are the twins' stepmom, I want us to be cordial. They love and admire you, and I appreciate you being a mother figure in their lives."

"I accept your apology and thank you. I do want us to be cordial. I respect your position as their mother. I would never disrespect that."

She smiles. "I know. So can we start over?"

"Yeah."

She outstretches her hand. "Hi, I'm Sasha, Ace and A'Mya's mom. Nice to meet you."

I accept her proffered hand. "Hi, I'm Tanya, Antwain's wife. Nice to meet you too."

I leave Sasha's house happy that we were able to come to an understanding. Dealing with ex's and coparenting don't have to be a problem if we as adults can be mature about the situation and do what's best for each other and the children involved.

I gave up on my faith and God once, I don't plan on doing that ever again. I'm beyond blessed, and I look forward to all the Lord has in store for me and my family. And right now, it's time for me to head back home to welcome my husband.

"And let us not grow weary of doing good, for in due season we will reap, if we do not give up." Galatians 6:9.

A message from the author:

Thank you for reading and making it to the end! That means you liked it, right? I ask one favor of you if you connected in any way with the characters – if you laughed, cried, if they broke your heart, or you cheered them on – ***please leave a review with no spoilers***. I would appreciate it greatly. Reviews are beneficial for authors to not only help us improve our craft and learn your likes and dislikes as a reader, but it also helps us connect with you. Take a few short minutes and leave a constructive review for me. Thanks!

Read you later! (Corny, I know. I couldn't help myself ▢)

Let's connect on Instagram:

@introvertedkhara

Follow me on Amazon so you always know when I have a new release.

Check out other titles by me if you haven't already (more on my Amazon Author Page) …